An Imprint of Sterling Publishing
387 Park Avenue South
New York, NY 10016

This 2014 edition published by Sandy Creek.

ISBN 978-1-4351-5468-1

Manufactured in Nansha, China
Lot #:
2 4 6 8 10 9 7 5 3 2 1
03/14

When I dream of

Sandy Creek
NEW YORK

Polar Bear.

Polar bears are big and white, and
can sometimes be a bit grumpy.
If you meet a grumpy polar bear,
build a funny snowman to cheer him up.

Wizards.

Wizards are jolly fellows with long gray beards and pointy hats. Wizards cannot hear very well on account of all the hair growing out of their ears.

Hippos.

Hippos have very sensitive skin
and love wallowing in oozy mud.
If you ever see a sunburnt hippo,
try not to laugh as this can make
it turn even redder.

Dinosaurs.

Dinosaurs are very good at hiding
and so everyone thinks they
are extinct. If you find a dinosaur
hiding under your bed, it is best to
sleep somewhere else.

Whales.

Whales are very, very big, and
have very deep voices. Always
stand back when a whale burps, as its
breath can smell rather fishy.

Pirates.

All pirates have pet parrots and
mostly wear pajamas. Pirates love
to fight and never say sorry.

Penguins.

Penguins like two things:
sliding and swimming. Because
they have large feet, they are
very good at both.

Teddy Bears.

Teddy bears are kind and cuddlesome. They meet up with their friends when you are asleep and like to eat custard sandwiches.

Ladybugs.

Most ladybugs are bright red with black spots. Despite their name, not all ladybugs are ladies, but it is hard to tell the difference.

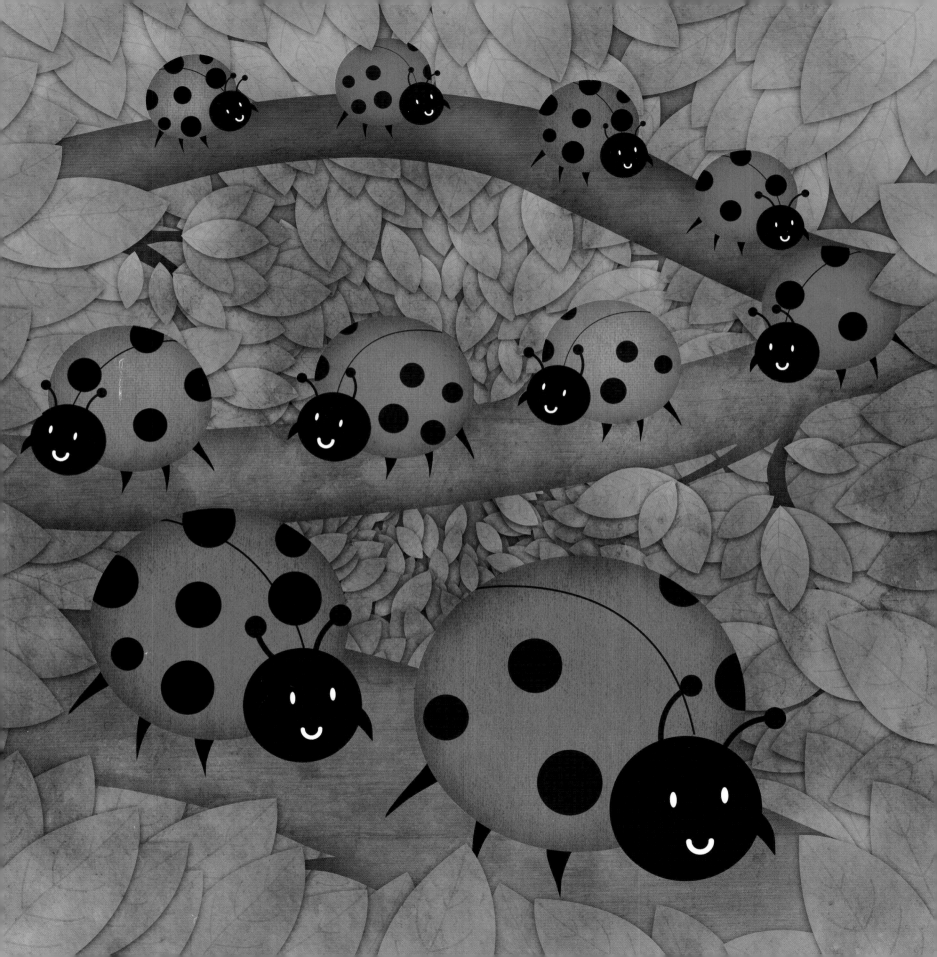

Meerkats.

Meerkats like eating crunchy bugs
and wrestling. Because of this,
their burrows tend to be rather messy.

12

Hot Air Balloons.

Flying in a hot air balloon is a wonderful adventure. Remember to always go to the bathroom before you take off, as it can take a long time to get down.

Dolphins.

Dolphins live in the sea and eat fish. Dolphins love to tell jokes and they brush their teeth three times a day.

Clouds.

Clouds come in lots of different shapes, colors, and sizes. Although they sometimes look fluffy and pink, they do not taste like cotton candy.

Sea Horses.

Sea horses like two things: swimming forward and swimming backward. Because they are rather small, they never get very far.

Pixies.

Pixies are the same size as
daisies and have lots of freckles.
If you are quick enough to count a pixie's
freckles, they will grant you a wish.

Diamonds.

Diamonds always sparkle and twinkle in the light. Most queens have lots of diamonds and get very cross if the king does not buy them more for their birthday.

Jellies.

Jellies are made from special wobbly ingredients. Despite being so wobbly, jellies don't fall over very often and taste great with ice cream.

Books.

Every book has a beginning, a middle, and an end. It is best to start reading a book at the beginning, followed by the middle, and then finish at the end.

Rabbits.

Rabbits have big, floppy ears and like to work with magicians. Make sure that you have a good supply of carrots if you invite a rabbit to a party.

Sheep.

Sheep look like fluffy clouds with legs. On account of sheep being rather boring, if you have trouble sleeping it is recommended that you try counting them.

40

Goblins.

Goblins are small and green and very naughty. Most goblins eat with their fingers and never say please or thank you.

Clownfish.

Clownfish do not dress in funny
clothes or do silly things to make
you laugh. Despite their name,
they are nothing like real clowns at all.

60

Ants.

Ants are very small and have lots
of brothers and sisters.
They are always busy and never
have time to go to parties.

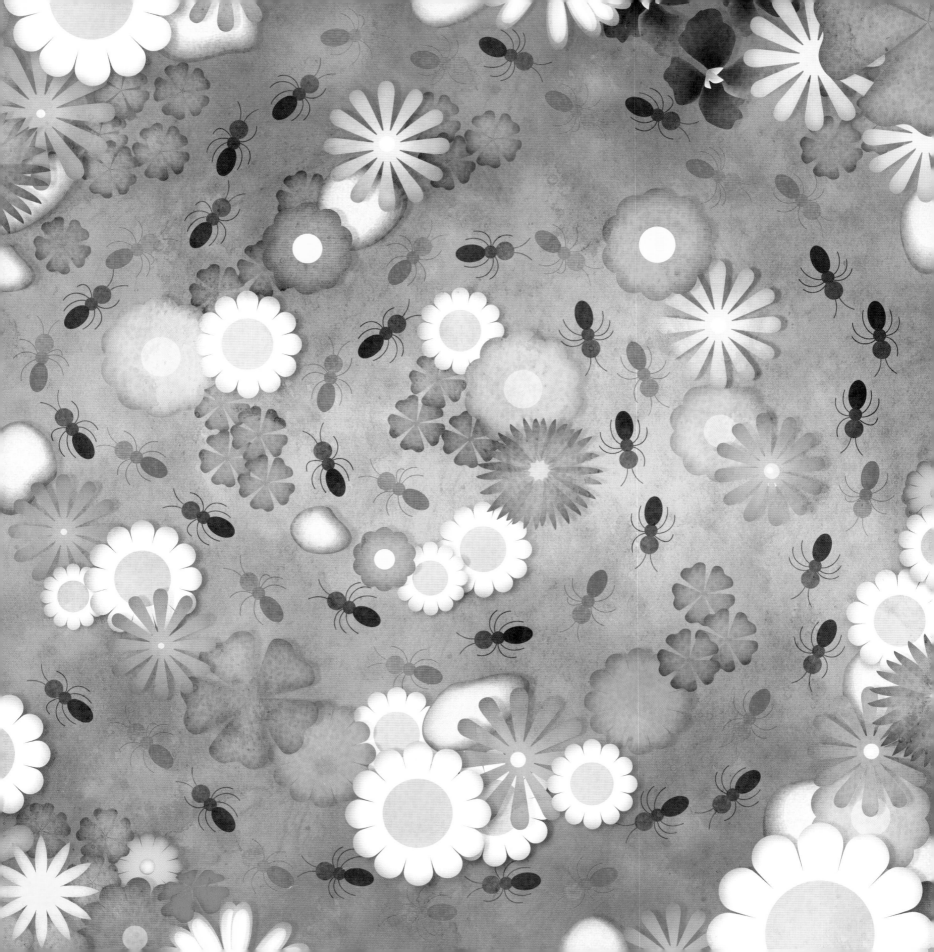

Snowflakes.

Snowflakes are cold and wet and can mostly be seen in winter. Snowflakes are a great invention and can be used to make fun things like snowmen and snowballs.

80

Raindrops.

Raindrops travel across the sky in clouds. When a cloud gets tired, the raindrops have to get off and fall to the ground.

90

Flowers.

A flower's main job is to look pretty and to feed the bees. Some flowers are quite mischievous and like to make people sneeze.

100

Stars.

When I dream of 123, I see twinkling stars. If you ever see a shooting star, close your eyes and make a wish.

Sleep tight and goodnight...